SPACE
ROCKS!

A Universe of Looney Verse

Written and Illustrated by

Ian Billing

&

Chris White

First published in Great Britain in 2011
by Caboodle Books Ltd
Copyright © Ian Billings and Chris White 2011

A Catalogue record for this book is available
from the British Library.

ISBN 978 0 9565 239 8 3

Cover and Illustrations by Ian Billings and Chris White
Page Layout by Highlight Type Bureau Ltd
Printed by Cox and Wyman

The paper and board used in the paperback by
Caboodle Books Ltd are natural recyclable products
made from wood grown in sustainable forests.
The manufacturing processes conform to the environmental
regulations of the country of origin.

Caboodle Books Ltd
Riversdale, 8 Rivock Avenue, Steeton, BD20 6SA
www.authorsabroad.com

CONTENTS

WELCOME ABOARD

Well – hello everybody
It seems everyone's inside.
We're all going on a Space Trip
You're welcome along for the ride.

But before we start – an announcement!
Health and Safety's important – so,
Before blasting into outer space
There's a few things that you need to know...

If this book should shoot into orbit any time
And zero-gravity rages,
You'll float up to the ceiling but please don't be sick,
Especially not on the pages.

And I hope you've all brought space helmets along,
As asteroids could hit, it's been said.
If you've not got a helmet – then take this book
And hold it over your head.

Get ready for a rip-roaring, rhyme-rocket ride,
Strap yourselves in, as instructed.
And hopefully we'll all make it through to the end
Without anyone being abducted...

SPACE STATION REGISTRATION

Aliens, please, pay attention!
Answer your names – or a light-year's detention.
Zorb? Zorkan? Zootle? Zim?
He's morphed again - Are you sure that's him?
Zardoz, Zoo-Zoo, Zindoz, Zen?
Zalex, Zander – late again?
Tell your mum she really oughta
get a faster teleporter!
Zag, please, I know you're the class clown,
but kindly put that ray-gun down!
Zorb, please, I know you're the class clone
but leave Zorkan's tentacles alone!
Zodon! Turn your eyes to me.
Yes, all six hundred and twenty-three.
Come down, Zog, I've got a feeling
you won't find your pencil on the classroom ceiling
You with the red finger, please, don't moan
I've told you twice – you can't phone home!
Now then, Zing, do you suppose
you could take the school pet out of your nose?
I know it's cute but it has fleas.
Don't point it at me! Please don't sneeze!

Aaaaaaachoooooo!

"Hello, Ground Control? Zing's done it again.
The school gerbil's orbiting sector ten!"
Zing, you really are a silly clot,
You might think it's funny, I think it's snot!

COUNTDOWN...

All is quiet, still – and then
the countdown starts with a massive TEN!
Way-out words wait in line
to hear an earth-shattering NINE!
Sonic phonics softly wait
with cosmic commas for the giant EIGHT!
Laser phrases point to heaven
It's rhyme-travel time – here comes SEVEN!
Pulsating poems, astrophysics
Supernovas and a humongous – SIX!
Full stops switch to hyper-drive,
exclamation sparks – it's a deafening FIVE!
Lock the windows, seal the door,
Fire up the apostrophes – here comes FOUR!
Start up the speech-marks, no time to flee
Open the book and shout out THREE
Find a poem, that's what you do
and stand by for the mighty TWO
Keep well back, the fun's begun
Galactical poetry – here comes ONE!
Cosmic rhyme for heroine or hero.
Fingers in ears – it's the final ZERO!

Brace yourself - it's time to cast off
Ten to zero – time to BLAST-OFF!

MCMARS

Welcome to McMars
That's right! Who knew?!
We've turned the whole of the planet
Into a space Drive-Thru!

Drive your spaceship over here
Pull up to the window – yeah you!
You haven't lived until you've tried
Our out-of-this-world menu!

There's a Big Bug Quarter Pounder
Made with squishy alien insects of course!
Try it with our Kosmic Ketchup
Or maybe some slozz noogle sauce!

Or perhaps you'd prefer a Filet o' Froggle
When you bite it – its eyeballs burst!
It might sound disgusting but don't worry we've
Taken most of its tentacles off first!

Or maybe you'd like a McPlopper Burger
Sink your teeth in and it'll go PLOP!
With a side order of Fnargle Flaa Flaa Fries
And asteroids sprinkled on top.

Would you like a special Wookie Whopper?
If you do just give me a shout!
These burgers take ages to eat
Coz you have to pick all the hair out...

Maybe some Nitro Beast Nuggets
But that will take a while you see
We have to chase the Nitro Beast round the kitchen
As he doesn't give up his nuggets easily!

Our Saturn Rings are fresh and crispy
Wash 'em down with Galactic Fizzy Glug
But please leave room for a portion of
Our Kentucky Fried Space Slug.

Please leave room for pudding! Our Solar Apple Pie
Isn't the most popular dish in the place
It's so hot in the middle – it's like biting the sun
And it'll end up melting your face.

And don't forget all our meals now come
With melted Hairy Blarg Blarg Cheese!
So welcome to McMars...
Can I take your order please??

DOLL ALIEN

I've got a dolly alien,
I keep her in a pram.
She's got a cute and pink smile.
She's as quiet as a lamb.

I know my doll's an alien
From a planet far away,
But I've dressed her in a nappy
And bib to make her stay.

I've taken both antennae
And hid them under her hat
And wrapped up all her tentacles
in her giant crawling mat.

I've put her in a romper suit
That suits her to a T!
Now she looks a lot more baby-like
And less like an ET

Today she said her first word,
It nearly made me cry.
The word she said was, "Mothership!"
and pointed at the sky.

Then there was a trembling
And light fell all around
My dolly was abducted
And her bib fell on the ground!

It was all a trauma
I shouted out, "Please stop!"
Then I shrugged and said, "Heigh-ho!
I'll get another one from the shop!"

SATURN SHOPPING MALL

Welcome to The Saturn Shopping Mall
We have everything you need and much more.
Come spend lots and lots in hundreds of shops
Located on every floor!

Fly your ship into our rocket park
It's multi-multi-multi-storey
With over three thousand levels
So parking's not a problem you see!

Girl creatures – if you love cosmetics
Visit Space Boots if you can
Or for the latest fashions Plu-Top Shop
For the boys – we have Top Space Man!

If fitness is your favourite thing
Our sports shops are pretty neat!
You'll find a cool pair of trainers, no matter
Whether you've two, four, eight or twelve feet!

Tired of shopping? Well, put your tentacles up,
In our food court, relax and feel fine.
If you just want a coffee, visit Shooting Starbucks
For a latte with cream and whipped slime.

Then how about popping into Stargos?
Where you choose from a laminated book
Then stand in the queue and in a light-year or two
Your purchase will appear with some luck.

Yes, all your needs under one roof!
You can stay here hour after hour!
You're protected whatever the weather
Even from a meteor shower!

So we hope to see all you shoppers soon!
You'll think we are the best!
Yes, Visit The Saturn Shopping Mall!
We run rings round the rest!

(For those who have gone to the dark side
Give our other centre a call
It's smaller but far more evil
Yes, why not visit Darth Mall)

THERE'S AN ALIEN IN MY POCKET

There's an alien in my pocket
with galaxies to conquer.
There's an alien in my pocket.
No, wait, it's just a conker.

There's an alien in my pocket,
from Planet Twong it's come.
There's an alien in my pocket.
No, wait, it's just some gum.

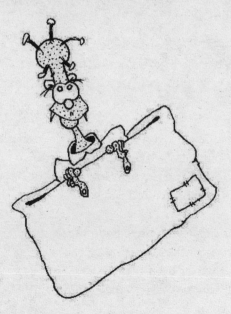

There's an alien in my pocket
with ray-guns, bombs and stuff.
There's an alien in my pocket
No, wait, it's just some fluff.

There's an alien in my pocket
I heard a ghastly groan
There's an alien in my pocket
No, wait, it's just my phone.

There's an alien in my pocket
His roaring engine's started
There's an alien in my pocket.
No, wait, it's me I've .... got to leave the room!

MIFFED MR. SHIFTER

One day on the Milky Way
a Shape Shifter failed to display
his skill to contort
at the speed of thought.
He sighed, "I'm just not myself today!"

BLIP BLIP BLIP

Flaaarp shnuggle blip blip blip
Sweedle teedle sqwidgey squip.
Boing boing Lady Ga Ga Poink!
Weeeee! Thwwpp! Aaaaaargggghhh!! Boink boink!!

I PANTS

You've heard of the i-pod.
You've watched the i-player.
You know the i-phone.
But they're so last year.

You've seen the new i-pad.
Well – here is your chance,
To now see the future...
I give you....i-pants!!!

Undergarments grubby?
Knickers quite dated?
Boxer shorts battered?
Y-fronts X-rated?

You'll no longer worry,
You won't have a care
When you have this 21st
Century underwear.

'So what do they do?'
You wonder out loud,
Well with i-pants you'll really
Stand out from the crowd!

They'll be no more tiresome
Pulling pants up and down.
With Voice Recognition,
There's no need to frown!

Just by saying 'Pants Down!!'
They shoot down your legs so,
It's ideal for those times,
When you've just gotta go!!

And i-pants are self cleaning,
You know it makes sense,
So wave goodbye everybody,
To those little accidents...

Then with a click of a button,
And no buts or ifs,
No more unsightly stains
Or slightly dodgy whiffs.

With a range of fab fragrances
You'll smell sweet once more!
Choose from vanilla, wet dog
Or taxi cab floor…

Another great feature
If you fancy a dance,
You can play all your music
By using i-pants!

Yeh! Turn up the volume!
You'll hear your favourite track,
Boom from a speaker
Positioned round the back!

i-pants are available,
in two colours – all right?
One for the boys,
In a slightly off-white.
And for the girls,
Pink and frilly were designed!
(Or I suppose for any boys
Who are that way inclined…)

There are many more features
If you're lost and alone,
With Sat Nav in the waistband
Your pants will guide you home!

Ring your friends on the phone
No matter where they are!
But we don't suggest texting,
As it looks quite bizarre…

How do I know they're so great?
How do I know? How?
Well, between you and me,
I'm wearing some now!!

Yes! i-pants are here!
i-pants make sense!
For only two thousand pounds,
And ninety-nine pence!!

i-pants are awesome!
The future is bright!
Please make out your cheques
To Billings and White.

And when you've paid all that money.
And you're not left with a dime,
We'll bring a better version out,
In a couple of weeks' time!!

VINDALOONATIC

An alien of which you will learn
Has a take-away place on Saturn
He sells rice and curry
To spacemen in a hurry
But careful, it doesn't half burn.

THE WEDGION

Beware the Wedgion, my friend,
He creeps up in the night,
materialises by your bed
and snaps your pants up tight!

He's such a vicious alien
causing so much pain.
When you turn your back on him
He tugs your pants again!

He really doesn't give a hoot
'bout what you say or feel.
He simply gives the wedgie,
stands back and lets you squeal!

He doesn't care who he attacks
as long as they have knickers.
He's wedgied three school-dinner staff,
a caretaker and some vicars!

The lollipop man was next in line
he shouted, "Eeeek!" and, "Stop!"
But the Wedgion wedgied him just the same
then stole his lollipop!

Beware the Wedgion, my friend,
You know last time he struck?
He wedgied all your teachers
then hung them on a hook!

So if you meet the Wedgion
you must do something drastic
like hide and run or shout out, "Mum!"
or he might snap your elastic!

MARTIAN AID

Save the Alien!
Save us from man!
Please donate!
Give what you can!

Save the alien!
Save E.T.!
Give all your money
Straight to me!

If people see us
They just scream
Then ring the police
Or the SWAT Team.

Next thing I know
I'm in a robe
Getting acquainted
With a long probe.

Some I'm told
(And this is the pits)
Get dissected
Into tiny bits.

So save the Martian
Give us a break
Treat us nicely
For goodness sake.

Make a Martian
Your friend today.
Don't just yell
Or run away

Help our charity
Come on, be quicker.
Give me a quid
And I'll give you a sticker.

THE BEAGLE HAS LANDED

Now, not many people know this –
but I'll give your memory a jog
Did you realise the first life form on the moon
was actually a dog?
His name was Beagle Armstrong –
the first space-dog of all time!
And he blasted off into outer space in the rocket
'Apollo Canine'.

Beagle sat in his pilot's seat – strapped in and
helmet strapped on
The countdown began – he closed his eyes…
10-9-8-7-6-5-4-3-2-1

BLAST OFF!! The rocket shot skyward –
Beagle's face turned a strange shade of violet.

But he wasn't alone – Buzz Budgie was there,
his wingman and trusty co-pilot!
Their mission was to visit the moon and set up a secret base.
Beagle's only worry was he'd heard there were no lamp posts
in outer space.

As they flew through the stars Beagle's astronaut training,
was running through his head.
He was trained in space travel, flying a ship and how to
shake a paw and play dead.
Both astronauts felt a touch space-sick as moonward
they hurtled still.
Beagle Armstrong coughed up a fur ball –
Buzz Budgie threw up some Trill.

Finally they arrived on the moon –
they found a space, then parked.
He got on the radio to mission control,
"THE BEAGLE HAS LANDED!" he barked.

They climbed down the ladder but it was broken –
it wouldn't fully unwind.
So while it was a small step for a dog – it was a giant leap
for budgie-kind.

They built their moon base and the pair moved in,
now feeling full of good cheer!
They tried to celebrate but the party was flat –
yep, there was no atmosphere.
Beagle unpacked his bowl, squeaky bone and dog chews
for good health.
Buzz Budgie put up a small mirror so he could talk
to himself.

It was soon time to return from their journey
into the unknown
But first Beagle wrote postcards to his doggy friends
back home.
They shot through the stars going back to Earth,
the journey lasted an age.
Beagle played 'Nintendogs' and Buzz slept a lot
with a blanket draped over his cage.

Apollo Canine landed to a cheering crowd –
both travellers feeling the strain
Beagle Armstrong felt a little dog-rough and
Buzz Budgie threw up again.

Crowds cheered – well, more like barked and yapped! They
were interviewed by newsmen
Beagle spoke about how very proud he was.
Buzz said, 'Who's a pretty boy then?'

And that is the tale of the first dog to go
where no dog has gone before.
Some say he was barking mad –
but he was over the moon for sure!

THERE'S AN ALIEN IN MY BEDROOM

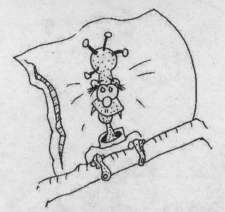

There's an alien in my bedroom
just sitting over there
I can see its evil alien eyes
and its vengeful little stare.

There's an alien in my bedroom
its fangs are sharp and spiky
It's going to creep and leap up on me
Oh, flipping heck and crikey!

There's an alien in my bedroom
I can see its spotty bum
It's going to tear me limb from limb
I really want my mum.

There's an alien in my bedroom
I can see its slimy sneer
step by step it's moving close
It's getting very near!

There's an alien in my bedroom
I can see its pokey nose!
No, wait, the light's come on.
It was just a pile of clothes!

SASHA THE SPACE UNICORN

Sasha the Space Unicorn
Gallops through the night sky
She is a lonely unicorn
And let me tell you why

There are no other space unicorns
Sasha's the only one
She has no friends to play with
They've all left and gone...

Until today – hip hip hooray!
Sasha's a smile on her face!
Rarely does she see, people like you and me
Floating out in space

But look – there is a spaceship
She can't disguise her joy!
It's full of folks who might be her friend
Be it girl, woman, man or boy!

Sasha's zooming towards the spaceship
A little too fast it must be said
Careful Sasha! Please slow down!
Don't forget that horn on your head!!

Sasha! NO! PLEASE STOP! WHOA!!
She careers into the ship's side
Her horn has pierced the hull and left
A hole two centimetres wide!

Everyone on board starts screaming!
"We're going down! ABORT THE MISSION!!"
Emergency sirens start wailing
They assume the crash position...

Sasha the Space Unicorn
Won't be making any friends today
She looks at the ship, blushes, mumbles, "Oops, sorry!"
Then quickly gallops away...

MOON ROCK

I've got a piece of Moon Rock
It's true, it's not a fiddle.
It is a stick of Moon Rock
It's got Moon written right through the middle.

DARK SIDE OF THE SPOON

An alien with a head like a balloon
Lives on the dark side of the moon
His face reminds me
Of what you will see
If you look in the back of a spoon.

THE TALE OF THE SAD BLACK HOLE

Let me introduce myself
I'm a very sad black hole.
My life is dull and boring
it's far from rock and roll.

I sit out in the galaxy
Light-years from the nearest sphere
and if anybody visits me
they simply disappear.

For I've a little problem
It's quite unmentionable
You see, I simply can't control
my gravitational pull!

If an alien is passing
and stops to say hello
suddenly they're sucked right in
and swallowed in one go.

Anyone who passes by
they cannot pull away.
They find me quite attractive
but not in the nice way.

The dentist came to visit me
and dentists make me wince
He filled a filling then fell in
I haven't seen him since.

The other day a visitor
was a Venusian with ice cream
I sucked the ripple off his cone.
You should have heard him scream.

The postman came a-calling
But there's that sucking sound
ten seconds later, all that's left
Are letters floating around

Planets, stars and comets
Get sucked and all go crunch
Not the ideal recipe
for an intergalactic lunch.

I was orbited by an asteroid
under close investigation
The asteroid got swallowed too
it's given me indigestion.

Now the asteroid's ticking -
it's the type that self-destructs!
I hate my life as a black hole.
Everything about it sucks!

PLANET OF THE PENGUINS

Welcome to Planet Penguin
It's like no place you ever saw
It's peculiar on Planet Penguin
Let me give you a guided tour.

As you can imagine – it's freezing here
The ground's covered with snow and ice
Some folks say it's too cold on our world
But we think it's very nice.

No penguin will ever complain of the cold
Well – having said that – not many
But you won't hear our knees knock or teeth chatter
Coz penguins don't have any...

We sometimes go out into space and explore
We visit other planets as day trippers
But it's tricky controlling complicated spaceships
When you've got no hands – just flippers!

And sometimes we discover new planets
In the universe below and above
Our penguin explorers always come in peace
And try to spread harmony and love.

Oh, except that time we found one world
We didn't half give 'em a scare!
You see we discovered The Planet of the Fish
And we ate everyone there.

And if you visit our planet
Just be careful as we are at war.
with The Planet of the Polar Bears
That unfortunately's next door.

So if you pop by – bring a jumper
some warm socks – a couple of pairs.
And a good pair of trainers so you can out-run
Any invading polar bears...

THERE'S AN ALIEN IN MY TOILET

There's an alien in my toilet
I hope it doesn't stay.
No, wait, I've just pulled the chain
and flushed it straight away!

PLANET OF THE HAMSTERS

Welcome to Planet of the Hamsters
First time? Let's give you the tour.
It's snuggly and warm on our planet
As it's covered with much fluff and straw.

You're welcome to have a look around
And if you feel thirsty or dehydrated
Please use one of our water bottles
which are conveniently located.

Why not visit one of our shops
To purchase all of your needs.
We take all major credit cards
Or piles of sunflower seeds.

Did you know our planet is hollow inside?
So moving's no problem at all!
We all pile inside and start running
It's a giant hamster ball!

HOW TO BUILD YOUR OWN UNIVERSE

If you think that science is dreary
try this lovely Big Bang Theory.
If you're bored or at a loss
why not build your own cosmos?

First you need an empty space
infinity long is just the place
then you simply have to scatter
a millions tons of cosmic matter.

Make some atoms very small
till you can't see them at all.
Next stir in a trillion masses
of functionally inert gases.

Then you merely have to glue
up a zillion stars or two.
Next you sprinkle in the mix
The Laws of Thermodynamics.

Now to start your planetary motion
what you need's a big explosion.
Crash and smash! Ka-bing! Ka-boom!
Let it rip! There's lots of room!

That really got your worlds revolving.
Look right there – that's life evolving.
Count you still have all your spheres
then cool for thirteen billion years.

Now you have to find a spot
for a very special pale blue dot.
Make it lush with lots of greenery
add some oceanic scenery.

After that you're nearly done
Just light it with a massive sun.
Now you've finally given birth
to a baby planet – name it Earth.

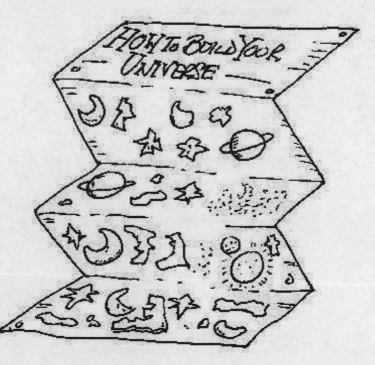

RE:PETE

There's a scientist alien called Pete
whose lab on Mars is quite sweet!
His experiments on time
And space were sublime
They caused all events to repeat

There's a scientist alien called Pete
whose lab on Mars is quite sweet!
His experiments on time
And space were sublime
They caused all events to repeat

There's a scientist alien called Pete
whose lab on Mars is quite sweet!
His experiments on time
And space were sublime
They caused all events to repeat

There's a scientist alien called Pete
whose lab on Mars is quite sweet!
His experiments on time
And space were sublime
They caused all events to repeat

There's a scientist alien called Pete
whose lab on Mars is quite sweet!
His experiments on time
And space were sublime
They caused all events to repeat

There's a scientist alien called Pete
whose lab on Mars is quite sweet!
His experiments on time
And space were sublime
They caused all events to repeat

There's a scientist alien called Pete
whose lab on Mars is quite sweet!
His experiments on time
And space were sublime
They caused all events to repeat

There's a scientist alien called Pete
whose lab on Mars is quite sweet!
His experiments on time
And space were sublime
They caused all events to repeat

NEIGHBOURS FROM OUTER SPACE

A family of aliens has moved in
They're living next door to us
They're the strangest family I've ever seen
But I'm trying not to make a fuss.

But they have their TV on really loud
I can hear it through the wall and COR!
They pick up channels with weird languages
Things I've never heard before...

When they're not watching their strange telly
They'll pop on a weird DVD
I can hear them hour after hour watching
'Independence Day' or 'E.T.'

Sometimes when we come home in our car
My dad has to bite his lip
As they've parked over the end of our drive
with their intergalactic spaceship.

If it is a hot day outside
I can see them trying to stay cool
I've never seen so many tentacles
Splashing around in a pool.

The next-door aliens keep me awake
And they give me a terrible fright
As sometimes they'll fire their laser guns
In the middle of the night.

And it seems they're getting bigger!
They grow and grow and grow!
You ought to see how many bags
they bring back from Tesco.

We might have to move out soon though
It really was the last straw
When Mrs Alien came round last night
And knocked on our front door.

"Goopy flub flub flager' she said
"Flooper glip glip flugger?"
Which roughly translated into English means
"Can I borrow a tanker full of sugar?"

PLANET GIRLIE

Planet girlie
Pink and swirly
Purple clouds
All curly wurly

Mermaids swimming
Princess slimming
Sparkly pop bands
All are singing

Ballet dancing
Prince entrancing
Silver shoes
And ponies prancing

Chocolate treat
Nice 'n sweet
This planet looks
Good enough to eat

I spoke too soon
Look at that spoon!
The planet's been eaten
By a space baboon!!

DARTH VADER'S GOT NO MATES

He's the most menacing in the universe.
He can get you with just a stare
If you look up evil in the dictionary
There's a picture of him in there...

Just the name DARTH VADER
Strikes terror in everyone's soul
His helmet and suit and flowing cape
Are as black as the blackest black hole...

But his diary's full of empty dates!
Coz Darth Vader's got no mates!

At Christmas he puts his decorations up
But no cards get sent to his home
Darth has no prezzies under his tree
He just sits and pulls crackers alone...

By the letter-box he waits!
Coz Darth Vader's got no mates!

He stands there in his front room
Looking like one sad Sith
Wiggling his arms around by himself
He's got no one to play Wii Sports with...

Yes – tennis is the game he hates!
Coz Darth Vader's got no mates!

Look at Darth in the playground
He's the loneliest Dark Lord in town
Sat on the end of the see-saw
That will never go up or down...

Sat crying behind the park gates!
Yes – Darth Vader's got no mates!

And there's Darth at his Birthday Party
He's got jelly, trifle and chocolate bars
Games ready to play like 'Pin the Tail on the Jedi'
And 'Musical Death Stars'...

But Darth sits, paper hat on his helmet
Staring at the door and the ground...
He wheezily blows his candles out and sobs
"Not even a Stormtrooper popped round..."

He's sat there with his paper plates
Yep, Darth Vader's got no mates!!

We don't really mean to make fun of you, Darth.
And I don't want to dis you ever
But maybe put your light sabre away
It's not big and it's not clever.

Perhaps don't blow so many planets up
or destroy things like you do
Just generally be a bit nicer
And you might make a friend or two...

THERE'S AN ALIEN IN MY TEACUP

There's an alien in my teacup,
Flipping heck! Good grief!
There's an alien in my teacup -
no, wait, it's just a (tea) leaf!

TO BOWLEDLY GO

This is Zilch the Goldfish
the first goldfish in outer space
See his shiny silver suit
and the smile upon his face.

He's conquered solar systems
but has one final goal
he wants to be the first goldfish
to visit a black hole

They put him in his space bowl
Made it nice and wet
Put his helmet on his head
and then the safety net.

But black holes are quite strange things
what wonders would he see?
They're dark, dim and peculiar
So full of mystery

The Boss stood and spoke out loud
"Zilch please pay attention
You're about to enter another world
beyond our own dimension!"

"You must record all you see
No matter how big or small
remember every detail -
you're a hero to us all!"

They launched Zilch just last Tuesday
he should be back real soon.
Wait! What's that over there
Zipping past the moon?

It's Zilch – he's heading earthward
what stories will he tell
of adventures beyond the stars
was it heaven or was it hell?

Zilch sits inside his space bowl
trying to catch his breath
looking like the goldfish
who just about cheated death.

They unscrewed his space helmet
green water seeping out
"Zilch , tell us, what did you see?
What is it all about?"

"Is it horrid? Is it nice?
Beautiful or rotten?"
Then Zilch spoke those famous words,
"I'm sorry, I've forgotten."

The moral of this story is
it might be a better plan
in future to launch an animal
with a wider attention span.

WHAT PLANET ARE YOU FROM?

You know, I guess, I reckon, I'm sure
It can't be true though...can it??
I think my little baby brother is
An alien from another planet.

The way he dribbles from his mouth
And it covers most of his face
That isn't normal is it?
He must be from outer space.

And the strange noises that he makes
He'll gurgle, squeal and blubber
A language I've never heard on this world
He has to be from another.

FURGLE GURGLE!

He'll wave his arms and legs around
I can't believe what I'm seeing!
These surely are the movements of
An extra-terrestrial being!

Even when he's fast asleep
And under his blanket he's curled
The smells that waft out of his baby-grow
Are really out of this world.

Then the way he crawls across the floor
Well what a weird feature!
Why doesn't he move like me or you??
He must be an alien creature!!

Hopefully, maybe, one day soon
My baby brother will be gone
When the mother ship lands to take him back
To whatever planet he's from.

BAA BAA SPACE SHEEP AND OTHER RHYMES

Hey diddle diddle, the cat and the fiddle
The cow jumped over the moon.
Wearing the latest hi-tech jet-pack
So she won't be back any time soon…

Humpty Dumpty sat on the wall
Humpty Dumpty had a great fall.
All the King's men said 'Ooh what a sight!
Humpty's been crushed by a meteorite!"

Baa Baa Black Sheep, have you any wool?
Yes sir, yes sir, three bags full.
One for the master and one for the dame
And one for the almighty galactic emperor Gurgle
who looks like a giant brain.

Little Miss Muffet sat on her tuffet
Eating her curds and whey.
An alien light
Beamed down in the night
And abducted Miss Muffet away…

Three blind mice, three blind mice
See how they run, see how they run
They put on their space-suits, went for a stroll
Tripped over their tails and began to roll
Got sucked into a massive black hole
Three blind mice.

Mary had a little lamb
Its fleece was white as snow
And everywhere that Mary went
The lamb was sure to go.

Then the lamb turned to the dark side
Mary said, "I'll save her!"
They battled for hours and in the end
The lamb was sheared with a light sabre.

Twinkle, twinkle, little star
How I wonder what you are
Up above the clouds so high
Like a diamond in the sky.

Sad your shining days were over
with that giant supernova!
A massive bang and then a tinkle
wiped the smile off your smug twinkle.

Oh dear, oh dear, oh little star
You're not as twinkly – not by far
If you recover from your attack
I hope you get your twinkle back.

SPACE BOOTS

A strange alien on Pluto
Bought himself a new suit-o
On one foot
A flipper he put
On the other, a Wellington boot-o.

DR. SEUSS'S THE TERMINATOR

I am a robot, I am, I am.
I am a robot, that I am.
I am a robot – machine legs and RAM.
Machine legs and RAM,
Machine legs and RAM,
I am a robot I am, I am.

The Rat in the Hat, the Rat in the Hat -
Time to engage in mortal combat!

Give me your hat, give me your hat!
Give me your hat, Rat in the Hat!

"No, no!" said the Rat, the Rat in the Hat,
"The hat stays on the rat!" That's that.
He couldn't compute what the Rat said,
So he took out his ray-gun and blew off his head!

PLANET PARTY

There's a Solar System Party tonight!
Everyone's invited
Mars is looking red hot
And the Moon is fully excited!

"I'm having such a great time!"
Mars to Saturn sings
Saturn's on the dance floor
Hula-hooping with her rings.

"Jupiter, make yourself useful!"
Earth loudly booms
"What's the point of being a helium planet
If you don't blow up the balloons?"

"I'll get started!" Jupiter sighs
And sits down, but didn't see
The smallest planet in the system
And squashed poor Mercury.

"It's freezing! Where's the heater?
Can we turn it up higher soon?"
"You're always the coldest planet around,
Put on a hat or a scarf, Neptune!"

"Who's that in the corner?" asks bruised Mercury
"That's Uranus" says Neptune. "It's known
That she is a gassy planet
So we make her stand there on her own."

Earth's gossiping with Mars about Venus
"Those volcanoes can't be good for her health!"
Jupiter is the largest planet
And scoffs half the buffet herself.

"LET ME IN GUYS!" – the music stops –
        everyone stares
"Can I enter?" says the voice at the door
"GO AWAY PLUTO!" the others all yell
"You're not even a planet any more!!"

Saturn spills a drink over Venus
Neptune eats Moon's sausage roll.
Jupiter criticises Saturn's earrings
The party slips out of control!

"STOP IT, YOU LOT!" The Sun rises up
"You heavenly bodies are a sight!
Why can't you all be a lot more like me?
Well behaved, charming and bright?"

The planets are ashamed, Earth whispers to Mars
"She's always causing a stir.
That's the trouble with the Sun, you know
She thinks everything revolves around her."

THERE'S AN ALIEN IN MY GARDEN

There's an alien in my garden
staring down at me.
There's an alien in my garden
No, wait, it's just a tree.

THE CHILLAX

A wonderful creature's the Chillax
sitting round doing nothing at all.
You may think that he's lazy
in fact, he's having a ball.

He'll sit in his bath for a millennium
never pulling the plug.
Blowing bubbles out of his ears
and drinking mud out of a mug.

He'll occasionally spend a decade
humming his favourite tune.
Once a year he'll brush his tooth
while waving at the moon.

A jolly thing's the Chillax
sitting on both his bums.
He'll happily spend the weekend
counting all his thumbs.

He's never had to question
The reason why he's here.
He just enjoys his simple life
year after year after year.

For the Chillax is immortal
He'll never die. No, never.
Just sit in his bath and chortle
for ever and ever and ever.

LIGHT SABRE'S LAST SWICH

Wom!Wom!Wom!Wom!
is the noise I have to make
Wom!Wom!Wom!Wom!
Shudder, shake and quake!

For I am a light sabre
the fiercest around
You can always tell a sabre
by its distinctive Wom!Wom! Sound.

Wom!Wom!Wom!Wom!
is the noise I have to make
Wom!Wom!Wom!Wom!
Shudder, shake and quake!

I've battled across the Cosmos
fighting clone after clone.
I've fought a million aliens
I've even surprised a drone.

Wom!Wom!Wom!Wom!
is the noise I have to make
Wom!Wom!Wom!Wom!
Shudder, shake and quake!

I've sliced my way 'cross Venus
Swashbuckled through many voids
I'm the kind of weapon
even a star ship avoids!

Wom!Wom!Wom!Wom!
is the noise I have to make
Wom!Wom!Wom!Wom!
Shudder, shake and quake!

But I've a little secret
Please keep it under your hat
I might be a mighty weapon
but my battery's going flat.

(slow)
Wom!Wom!Wom!Wom!
is the noise I have to make
Wom!Wom!Wom!Wom!
Shudder, shake and quake!

No splicing and no slicing
I think I'm going to cry
I just wish for one more swish
before I finally die...

(slower)
Wom! Wom! Wom! Wom!
My battery life is ending
Wom! Wom! Wom! Wom!
My massive light is bending..

...I'm fading and I'm drooping
...No longer got much clout
...power pack is failing
...and my little light's gone out.

(slowest)

Wom! Wom! Wom! Wom!
...no longer ....can defend
Wom! Wom! Wom! Wom!
...this really is .... the end....

Click!

Wait a sec, I'm feeling...
as powerful as a rocket
They've run an extension cable
and plugged me in a socket!

Again I can start womming
Wom! Wom! from star to star
But it's only a short extension
So I can't wom very far.

CLOSE ENCOUNTERS OF THE ABSURD KIND

Captain's Log: Stardate 3010
Reporting my latest find
I've bumped into an alien and had
A close encounter of the absurd kind.

This life form's like nothing I've seen before
It just looked really wrong
I knew it was strange as I went to shake hands
But he wanted me to shake his tongue.

I showed him my I.D. badge
Just so he would know
He didn't read it with his eyes
But with his left big toe.

I studied him a bit closer
Imagine my surprise!
This alien gurgled something like 'Hello!'
But by blinking both of his eyes!!

And then, you won't believe it
It had me nearly in tears!
This extra-terrestrial leapt in the air
And sneezed loudly through his ears!!

A rumbling noise? What was it??
He was hungry and I had to stare
As the alien took off his hat
And ate a sandwich with his hair!!

Then, oooh, what was he doing?
I couldn't believe what I was seeing!!
He took off his glove and heavens above!
The alien's thumb was peeing!!

And that was my encounter
With a thing from far-off lands
It gurgled, "Good Day! I'll be on my way…"
Then ran off on his hands…

THERE'S AN ALIEN IN MY LAPTOP

I've just downloaded an alien.
He's found out where I am.
I've just downloaded an alien.
No, wait, it's just some spam.

PRINCESS OF THE UNIVERSE

One day I'll be Princess of the Universe!
Everything will be just as I think
I'll get rid of the really dull colours
Everything will be lilac and pink!

I'll control every planet in the galaxy
They'll all be owned by me
And every shop in which I'll pop
Will give me cool clothes for free

Wherever I go in my pink spaceship
Everyone will do as I say
Nobody will walk –
we'll skip and dance
And my favourite songs will play

I'll write my name across the sky
Using twinkly stars
I'll bin all yucky food and just have
Milk shakes and chocolate bars

What a beautiful Princess of the Universe I'll be
With painted nails on my hands and toes
But until that day – I'll do as my parents say
And tidy up my room I suppose

BEHOLD THE MIGHTY QUONGO

Behold the Mighty Quongo
There's simply no one worse
The maddest, baddest alien
throughout the universe!

Behold the Mighty Quongo
He'll fight for all he's worth
He's dreaming up a scary scheme
He's invading Planet Earth.

He lands his ship near Tesco
strides round looking tough
He makes confronting grunting sounds
until he's had enough.

He points his sonic ray-gun
at every passerby
"Take me to your leader!"
you might just hear him cry.

"I claim this world for Quongo!"
He rummages in his bag.
"I am the King of Planet Earth!"
He shouts and plants a flag.

But no-one seems to hear him
No, nobody at all.
Do you suppose it's because
he's a millimetre tall?

"I am the Mighty Quongo,
Don't make me pull the trigger!
Oh, I give up! I'm going home!
But I'll come back when I'm bigger!"

ARE WE NEARLY THERE YET?

We're shooting through the stars
In our spaceship that we have
Dad's driving at warp speed one hundred and ten
And Mum's fiddling with the Sat Nav.

I'm in the back seat, staring outside
To see what I can see
And all I can hear is my baby sister
Sat right next to me...

"ARE WE NEARLY THERE YET?"

Whooooosh! A shower of meteors roars past
Oooh! Look at those funny things!
Wow! I think that's Saturn over there
Yep! I can see all of the rings!

Cor! There is a space-station!
Look! There's Pluto! Gee whizz!
I wonder what I'll see next?
What a fantastic flight this is!

"ARE WE NEARLY THERE YET?"

CRIKEY! An alien UFO!
That's like nothing that I've ever seen!
AAAARGGHHH! It's firing right at us!
We've been hit by a laser beam!!

"ARE WE NEARLY THERE YET?"

This is an incredible journey!
Now we're in a black hole miles wide!
I've never been in one of these before!
Whhooooosh! We're out the other side!

"ARE WE NEARLY THERE YET?"

We've shot out of the black hole into
The mouth of a massive Space Beast!
Thrusters on to escape his jaws
Before we end up its feast!!

"ARE WE NEARLY THERE YET?"

That place over there! What is it?!?
I've discovered an unknown world!!
AAAARRRRGHHH! WAIT! We've been hit by an
asteroid!!
And towards the sun we've been hurled!!!

"ARE WE NEARLY THERE YET?"

We're spinning towards the boiling sun!
Spinning out of control I fear!
We're going to burn into pieces!
It looks like the end is near!!

"ARE WE NEARLY THERE YET?"

Phew! We swerved at the last moment!
And I think we're going to survive!
I can't believe it! What a close shave!
I've never felt so alive!!!

"ARE WE NEARLY THERE YET?"

I've seen a black hole and meteors!
An unknown world and an alien ship!
And now we've docked at our destination
WHAT A RIDE! WHAT A TRIP!!

"ARE WE NEARLY THERE YET?"

"YES! YES! YES!!!."

"CAN WE GO HOME NOW?"

TEACHER™

OPERATING INSTRUCTIONS

Thank you for purchasing THE TEACHER™
Please follow the following fully...

KEY FEATURES

1 Sees things in your pocket like gum or elastic
2 Beware of this part (may be loud or sarcastic)
3 Can hear things up to ten metres away
4 May need wiping on a very cold day
5 Can be greasy, oily or dry
6 Can't play football but will often try
7 Skin comes smooth or smothered with zits
8 Beware of these fast moving bits

DANGER
DO NOT ATTEMPT TO REMOVE THE COVER
OR LOOK AT THE WORKINGS

INSTALLING YOUR TEACHER™
Unpack, very carefully then place on a chair,
(Make sure no one's left a drawing pin there)
Remove the coat, the scarf and the hat,
Then wind-up your TEACHER™ and hear it chat.

WARNING
NEVER WIND-UP YOUR TEACHER™ TOO MUCH.
IT MAY CAUSE DAMAGE

CARING FOR YOUR TEACHER™
Wipe only with a dampish rag
And if your TEACHER™ starts to sag
Pat its head and then insert
A spoonful of a nice dessert.

CLOSING DOWN YOUR TEACHER™

To close down your TEACHER™ is very simple
You have to locate its on/off dimple.
But wait until the end of the day,
Give it a prod – and then run away.

MOST IMPORTANT!

KEEP YOUR TEACHER™ OUT OF REACH OF
CHILDREN FIRST THING IN THE MORNING.

LITTLE GREEN MAN

I'm the Little Green Man who comes from Mars.
Speeding past the cosmic stars
using astronomic power
to travel a million miles an hour.
Swerving, curving, dipping, diving
Spinning planets with my driving
Sliding, gliding, mega-swooping,
Slipping, zipping, loop-the-looping
I travel the heavens double quick
I'm not usually green - I'm just travel sick.

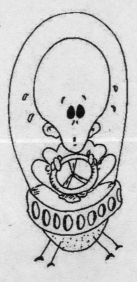

MY WORLD IS FULL OF ALIENS

My world is full of aliens
I see them everywhere
in my house and my bed
and in my underwear.

They break into our atmosphere.
What are they trying to find?
Is it true or is it my
over-active mind?

Are they trying to contact us
from another dimension?
Or is it just a trick of the light
plus my (mad) imagination?

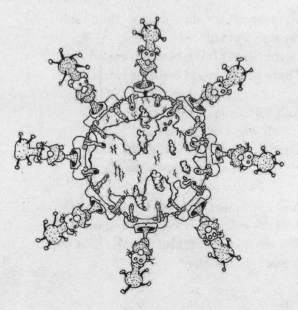

WELCOME TO EARTH

Greetings to you Earthlings
Please don't call the police.
For although I am an alien
Chill out! I come in peace!

I've been among you a week or two
Having a look round the place
And one thing I've learnt about humans is
You're not half a funny race!

On my planet, the weather is gorgeous
It's so warm but here it's yucky.
It seems to rain all the time
Apart from one week in June if you're lucky.

Up in space my ship is faster than light
Zipping from place to place
Down here it takes hours to get anywhere
There are no speed cameras in space.

And I find your money confusing
It's all very strange to me
There's some coins and paper – but as far as I can tell
Nectar Points are your currency.

And I've learnt that you humans love football.
And the rules, they seem quite fair,
The most successful team is the first to find
A Saudi billionaire

On my world we have many fine foods
So much choice – I lick my green lips!
Here on Earth it seems you'll eat anything
As long as it's served up with chips.

Yes – I quite like it here – I may stay a while
Before back through the cosmos I'm hurled.
Your weather is lousy – your food is quite gross
But your poetry's out of this world!

SYDNEY STARBUCK IN CLOSE ENCOUNTERS OF THE FURRED KIND.

The bread sat in the toaster, the clock said 8:04
As Sydney Starbuck yawned and heard his mail
drop through the door.
In amongst the usual bills, one letter looked exciting.
Sydney thought – "Now, who's this from?
I don't recognize the writing. . ."

The envelope was reduced to shreds - a letter was inside
And as he read it Sydney's eyes and mouth were open wide.
Two words - "JOB" and "INTERVIEW" leapt at him
from the pages
And Sydney's mind flashed back to the last time
he'd earned some wages...

It had certainly been a long while
since Sydney had enjoyed,
The money and the benefits that come
from being employed.
Had it only been two days ago that
Sydney Starbuck had,
been flicking through his paper
and seen the tiny ad. . .

... *"Wanted: Man, who's good and true and always keeps his word,*
To be defender of the Earth. (Experience preferred)"
The ad went on: *"We're looking for someone immediately..."*
So Sydney sent a letter off - enclosing his C.V...

Now here was Sydney Starbuck -
a no one, nothing, zero,
On the verge of being made
a full-time super hero! ! !
Sydney grabbed the telephone -
asked for the right extension,
Then was asked to hold the line...
he couldn't bear the tension...

. .. After twenty minutes or so of listening to Boyzone,
A voice woke slumbering Sydney up - screeching down the phone.
"Mr.Starbuck? Sorry to keep you - thanks for ringing so soon.
We'd like you to come in today. Are you free this afternoon?"

"Ok!" blurted Sydney "I'll be there in a bit!
See you later! Bye!"
Then dashed off to dust down his solitary suit
and find a shirt and tie.
A couple of hours later and
Sydney looked supreme.
His shoes were shined, his teeth were brushed,
his hair dripped with Brylcreem.

"I need this job!" thought Sydney,
"There's nothing l want more!"
The bread still sat in the toaster
as he dashed out of the door...
"Bbbbzzzz! !" Went the buzzer, "Come in!" came the call
- so Sydney Starbuck did,
Whistling softly to himself "You can do this Syd...!"

Sydney looked across the room
to where a man was sat,
"Please take a seat" he stood and said,
"and we'll have a little chat!"
"Let me introduce myself - Mr. Black's the name,
I work for Grimsville Council
and I hope you'll do the same"

"My department is top secret - it's not roads or council tax.
We're responsible for stopping any alien attacks.
These attacks are happening all the time, why only the other day,
An alien sneaked up on the tea boy - and carried him away! !"

"We can't stop them from abducting - we've passed a law to ban it!
But obviously Grimsville Council has no power on their planet...
We're not even sure which planet they're from
and we don't know what's their plan.
We just know someone should stop them -
and you could be that man! ! !"

"You'll get a company space ship and a blaster of your own
And if I pull a few strings - how about a mobile phone??
Someone has to defend us - we've not a lot of time,
Here - just give me your details and sign on the dotted line. . ."

Mr. Black handed to Sydney
a chunky fountain pen.
Sydney browsed the form over -
was about to sign, but then...
Bursting through the flimsy wall
in a shower of wood and plaster,
Came a great big blob with one huge eye
and a state of the art blaster.

"SNARGLE - SLURP - BOOGLE! !" the alien yelled.
The two men froze where they stood.
Sydney hadn't a clue what it said but he knew it wouldn't be good.
The alien blob stuck a tentacle out and using its power of suction,
Grabbed Mr. Black and oozed back through the wall:
A text book alien abduction.

Sydney couldn't believe his luck – "My only chance of a job,
Has just been whisked off into space by a slimy alien blob!
I'm not going to let them get away with this!
I'm gonna save Mr. Black!
Let's see how the aliens like it when,
Sydney Starbuck strikes back! ! !"

He dashed into the car park
but was just too late to stop,
The alien ship from blasting off
over the fish and chip shop. . .
Sydney surveyed the car park and saw,
parked to his right,
A Grimsville County Council ship
that looked ready for flight.

Syd jumped into the driver's seat,
grabbed the wheel and took the brake off.
Then pressed the red ignition pad. . .
and waited for the take off. . .
. . . Twenty minutes later
Sydney was still sat there,
Hammering on the dashboard
and pulling out his hair.

"Come on! Move you pile of junk!"
as he pushed *"Ignite"* once more.
At this point, I'm afraid; I have to report,
that Sydney Starbuck swore!
Then suddenly, (we don't know why),
the engines spluttered and ignited
Sydney slid his seat belt on -
sat back, and got excited. . .

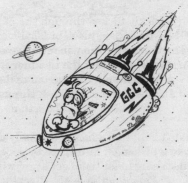

The space ship shot into the sky - fire screaming from its rockets.
Sydney felt his eyeballs rattling round inside their sockets.
The ship had reached the ozone in less than half a minute.
There was no problem getting through - there was a big hole in it. .

Before Sydney could catch his breath,
he was cruising through the stars,
To his right he could see Jupiter, to his left the planet...
oh sorry no - it's Saturn!
As the ship sped at the speed of light into outer-space,
Sydney thought, "How on Earth do I find this alien race?! !"

Sydney peered through the windscreen
looking for a clue,
But saw nothing but lots of space
and didn't know what to do.
Out came his Galaxy A to Z - but -
no alien location.
Just toilets, a Post Office plus
an old Russian space station. . .

Then. . . a beeping from the dashboard
and a light flashed on a pad,
"What does that mean?" Sydney thought
"Is it good or is it bad?"
Syd reached into the glove box
and had a little look
At the official *GRIMSVILLE COUNTY COUNCIL
SPACE SHIP HAND BOOK.*

As he quickly flicked through the pages,
Sydney didn't look outside-
So didn't see the space station about fifty-metres wide!
"CLAAANGGG! ! !" went the two space ships –
Syd's head sprang up to find,
He'd had a close encounter of the collision kind...

Slowly lowering the handbook, Sydney thought, "You twit!
Nothing but space for miles and miles
and I've found something to hit!
I can't believe I've got myself in such a situation.
I must go swap insurance details
with the driver of the station."

Sydney grabbed his space suit and got changed with great haste.
The suit wasn't a bad fit - just a bit tight round the waist.
Meanwhile - inside the space station, the aliens yelled
"WHAPOOOR!"
Which roughly translated means something like -
"There's somebody at the door!"

One little furry ball of hair -
about three feet in height,
Went scuttling passed huge computers
and banks of flashing lights. . .
He finally reached the entrance hatch -
pressed a switch - it started raising.
The alien thought, "I hope it's not
someone else selling double glazing."

"Good morning! The names Starbuck!
I come in peace my friend!
Oh - and I've also rammed your vehicle.
It shouldn't take long to mend!"
The alien looked Sydney up and down
looking quite dismayed.
"I can't believe it" the fur-ball said,
"We've just had it re-sprayed!"

"I'll send some troops to look at it and see what they all think,
In the meantime - come in - get comfortable -
would you care to have a drink?"
"That would be nice" replied Sydney
and the alien disappeared,
Sydney lowered himself into a chair and
thought something was weird...

Back came the furry alien - carrying a drink.
It was bright red glop with foam on top
and a terrible, terrible stink.
"Bottoms up!" the alien toasted,
"Good health to you and me!
I hope you enjoy this Spango drink -
(it's my mum's own recipe!)"

Sydney smiled and took a swig - then choked and spat it out.
It drenched the fur-ball, who started to bubble
and wildly thrash about!!
It flipped itself onto its back and a startling change took place. . .
It grew and grew, sprouted tentacles too
and a big eye in the middle of its face! ! !

"I recognize you!" yelled Sydney
you're one of those vile scum,
Who abducted my friend Mr. Black!
Well - now your time has come! !"
Sydney grabbed his council blaster
that was strapped to his left leg,
"If you had knees - then now's the time
to get on them and beg! !"

The alien snarled and slid away - Sydney gave pursuit
But found it quite hard to run very fast
in his Grimsville Council suit.
Syd charged down the corridors gripping his blaster tight.
Looking for an alien - and looking for a fight!

Suddenly, a hatch whooshed up and into the corridor was led,
Mr. Black - with the alien pointing a blaster at his head! !
"FNARGLE-THEW-SNARGLE-IKEA-WAPOO!"
the alien blurted out.
Syd said, "I wish you'd speak English -
I've no clue what you're on about! !"

"I said - prepare to say bye to your friend.
I'm going to blast him good
And then I'll suck his brains out - like any proper alien should! !"
Sydney aimed his blaster, smiled a confident smirk-
Pulled the trigger of his council gun...but it didn't actually work...

"Oh, yes!" Mr. Black said,
"The blasters - we'd had trouble with a few.
I was going to send an email round - it's on my list of things to do!"
Syd pressed the trigger again and again -
but it didn't do what it should.
"How am I to defend the Earth if my blaster is a dud?"

"I must think quickly - no time to lose -
come the hour, cometh the man!"
He checked his pockets and found something -
Sydney Starbuck had a plan! !
The alien stood, tentacles waving, blaster pointing at Mr. Black.
Sydney surveyed the state of play and knew it was time to attack. .

In one lightning quick motion, Sydney launched through the air,
Something that pierced the alien's eye
and was left stuck and wobbling there!
The alien writhed in agony - its tentacles flailing around.
The eye exploded in one gooey mess - then it fell -
quite dead - to the ground.. .

"WAHOOOO! !" cried Sydney, "I did it! The alien threat is gone!
Abducting alien scum - nil. Sydney Starbuck – one!"
Sydney grabbed the stunned Mr. Black, "Quick let's get out of here!
To the spaceship as quick as we can before any more appear!"

The spaceship started first time -
they sped away from the alien sortie,
As Sydney praised the Lord above for his can of WD-40.
Safely in the spaceship - blasting through the sky,
Mr. Black asked Syd,
"What exactly did you thrown in the alien's eye?"

"Well sir. . . " started Sydney, "Although I tried -
my blaster wouldn't save me,
And all I had in my pocket was this fountain pen you gave me.
The one I was using to fill in the form -
I thought it was worth a try. . .
I launched it like a dart - and you could say I hit bull's-eye!"

"It's lucky I had it on me or there could
have been a disaster!
So I suppose it's true what people say -
the pen is mightier that the blaster!"
"Mr. Starbuck,'' Mr. Black slowly said -
wiping his face free from blob,
"I think it's safe to say -
congratulations - you've got the job!"

Sydney sat back feeling warm and proud
as back to earth they roared...
"Now all that's left," he thought to himself,
"Are celebrations, medals and reward.
There'll be crowds of people, ticker-tape parades,
and a statue built with some luck.
I might even get a poem about me in a best-selling poetry book!"

Back in Grimsville the spaceship touched down
on the County Council car park
There were no screaming crowds or flag waving.
It was cold. It was rainy and dark.
I'm afraid Sydney wasn't treated like Han Solo or Captain Kirk...
He was stuck at his desk for the next fourteen days,
completing the paperwork...

The End